Splat the Cat
On with the Show

Based on the bestselling books by Rob Scotton
Cover art by Rick Farley
Text by Annie Auerbach
Interior art by Loryn Brantz
SCHOLASTIC INC.

For Gabriella

ISBN 978-1-338-35547-5

Copyright © 2013 by Rob Scotton. All rights reserved. Published by Scholastic Inc., 557 Broadway, New York, NY 10012, by arrangement with HarperFestival, an imprint of HarperCollins Children's Books, a division of HarperCollins Publishers. SCHOLASTIC and associated logos are trademarks and/or registered trademarks of Scholastic Inc.

12 11 10 9 8 7   22 23

Printed in the U.S.A.   40

First Scholastic printing, November 2018

Typography by Rick Farley

Splat and his classmates were getting ready to perform the school play, *Cinderpaws*. Backstage was a flurry of fur as the cats put on their costumes. Splat was so excited to be performing, he had butterflies in his tummy.

"Let the show begin," announced Mrs. Wimpydimple.
The curtain rose and the lights grew bright.
Kitten, dressed as Cinderpaws, was busy sweeping the floor.

Poor Cinderpaws. Her stepmother and stepsisters were very mean to her.

"Clean the floor! Sew this dress! Clean the floor *again*!"

When a royal ball was announced, Cinderpaws was left at home. She cried and cried.

Suddenly there was a puff of smoke, and her Fairy Godmouse appeared.
(It was really Seymour!)

The Fairy Godmouse magically changed Cinderpaws's rags into a beautiful dress.

Next, the mice were changed
into horses. They pulled a grand
carriage to the ball.

Backstage, Spike was
changing, too.

There was a *big* problem. Spike was about to make his grand entrance as Paw-Prints Charming, but he had stage fright.

"I can't go on! I'm not feeling well. I've got a bad case of the spots!" wailed Spike. He pointed at some purple spots on his face.

"Oh, dear!" said Mrs. Wimpydimple. "What *will* we do?"
Suddenly, Kitten had an idea. "What about Splat? He could play Spike's role."

Splat's tail wiggled with worry. He wasn't sure he could do it.

Splat looked at Kitten smiling at him. He didn't want to disappoint her.
So with all his courage, Splat said yes! He'd play the part!

A quick costume change,

and Splat was now Paw-Prints Charming!
The costume wasn't exactly a perfect fit, though.

The royal ball scene began.
Paw-Prints Charming bowed. "May I have this dance?"
Cinderpaws accepted and the music began.

The pair danced and danced until . . .
DONG! DONG! DONG! The clock struck
midnight and Cinderpaws ran away.

Splat tried to chase after her but tripped over his oversize costume!

He smashed into Plank the clock!

He grabbed the curtain and ripped it down.

Then everything went tumbling . . . *SPLAT!*

The crowd gasped.

What a complete mess!
Splat was really worried. "Mrs. Wimpydimple is going to be *so* mad at me."

The audience erupted in laughter and cheering.
"Bravo!" they shouted. "Encore!"
The show was a comedy hit!

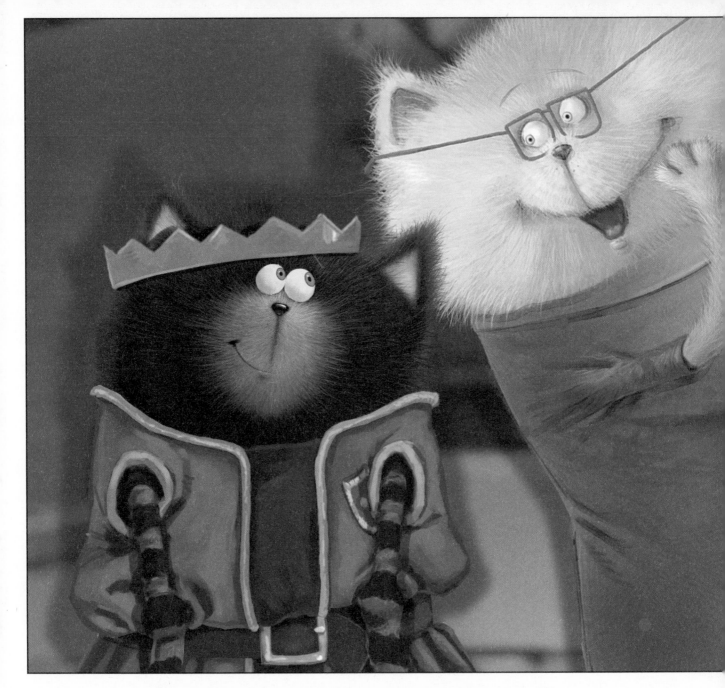

Mrs. Wimpydimple leaned in and whispered, "Do you think you can do that again tomorrow night, Splat?"